# A GIFT TO THE VIGO COUNTY PUBLIC LIBRARY

# Chef Yasmina

## AND THE
## POTATO PANIC

# Chef Yasmina

## AND THE
## POTATO PANIC

WAUTER MANNAERT

First Second
New York

One year later...

Eggplant stuffed with couscous, carrots, pear, and pumpkin

INGREDIENTS
2 eggplants
1 pear
1 lemon
3 carrots
300 g parmesan
1 shallot

clang

TUTTi FRiTTi

yasmina!

I'm home!

12

15

16

22

23

25

28

29

34

37

BROOAA

Boohoohoo!

?!

Boohoohoohoo!

Cyril!
Marco!

Oh, Yasmina, it's terrible!

Sniff!

When we arrived this morning to work in the garden, everything was gone! There wasn't a single plant left standing!

THEY LEVELED IT ALL!

46

BURP

DRííING

BROOOAAR

TOMATOES
2.80/kg

Can I help you, young lady?

No thanks! My dad's waiting! Bye!

A little while later...

58

60

cling
cling
cling
cling

The next morning...

111

118

128

139

T he idea for *Chef Yasmina and the Potato Panic* was born in 2009 while I was working on an art project with children in Brussels, the city in which I live. The goal for the children was to portray their daily lives with photos and videos. My job was to help them as needed.

On one of our walks we wandered over a large piece of fallow land—a real wilderness in the middle of the city. We stumbled upon a small iron gate hidden in the bushes. What we found behind it was a real surprise: a beautiful vegetable garden! With a little imagination, the city disappeared altogether. We might as well have ended up somewhere in the countryside.

The children and I stole some raspberries from the garden and stood in awe before an artfully constructed geodesic dome. Then we were off again, looking for the next treasure.

It was by no means the only vegetable garden I discovered that summer. In fact, it looked like everyone in town was gardening. And not only in the derelict parts of the city: balconies and rooftops were also transformed into vegetable gardens. And if those spaces were not available, people found their own solutions. Plastic bottles hanging in a window or wooden boxes on a sidewalk can also be used to grow beans or tomatoes.

Around the same time, Belgium had what the press called "the potato war of Wetteren." A group of activists destroyed a field trial of genetically modified potatoes at Ghent University. The activists, who opposed the introduction of genetically modified crops into our agricultural system, stormed the field and destroyed the work of the scientists.

It became clear to me that how and what we eat is an important topic in my community. Two basic questions were at the center of it: Should we trust science to solve the problems that confront the global food supply? Or should we go back to basics and rely on the immense diversity that nature offers?

I don't have the answers, but the questions kept me busy. And I started to dream along with those city gardeners who not only asked questions, but decided to create their own solutions. I planted some herbs on my balcony, a cherry tree in a pot on the terrace, and a few tomato plants in the living room. After a long wait and a lot of watering I was able to pick my own handful of cherries and three tomatoes. Yum!

But it was not enough. In my imagination it was all much bigger and more exciting. Slowly, a story about vegetable gardens, evil potato farmers, and Yasmina—the best eleven-year-old cook in town—started to take shape.

Now, ten years later, you can finally read the result. And I sure hope it tastes good!

—Wauter Mannaert
February, 2019

Here are some early concept sketches of Yasmina and her father in watercolor. I first imagined Yasmina much younger and with a strawberry hat. I also had the crazy idea to do the whole book in red and blue. Maybe not the best choice for a book about food and plants!

One of the first scenes I imagined was the one where Yasmina steals vegetables from her mysterious neighbor, Amaryllis. The kitchen knife and the retro ski cap give her something of a ninja look. Also visible: a first attempt to find a name for the bad guy in my story. Pal Parade is an anagram for aardappel (potato in Dutch). In the end I went for Tom de Perre, a variation on pomme de terre (the French word for *potato*).

I saw Yasmina as a busy bee—constantly running and cooking.

Here Yasmina's appearance gets close to the final version, with her white chef's hat and its little fork. In Belgium, french fries come with a colorful little plastic fork. I thought it was funny to stick one in her hat, like her own personal insignia.

Tom de Perre went through many transformations before I arrived at his final appearance. Here are just a few of the many sketches I did for this character. You can also see some of my sketches for the logo of his company, Project Potato: a stylized potato plant that transformed into a skull once he got his hands on it.

Before *Chef Yasmina and the Potato Panic*, I made a graphic novel about Weegee, an American photographer who worked in New York in the 1940s. With Yasmina, I wanted to stay away from the archives and find inspiration closer at home. I live in a very culturally diverse neighborhood in Brussels with beautiful houses from the early twentieth century. You can find this building around the corner from where I live. It houses a small Russian grocery store of some kind.

This is how I "write" my stories. At this stage, I draw as small as possible (every page is drawn in a 2.5 x 3–inch frame). This includes text and lots of details. Quite often I'm the only one who can read what's going on!

*Chef Yasmina and the Potato Panic* was my first comic in color (up until then I always worked in black and white). It quickly became clear watercolor wasn't the right medium for this book. This is the drawing where I first found a coloring technique I was happy with: a mixture of digital colors and brush pen (the blue shadows are the brush pen). It's fun to do and fits my sketchy drawing style.

First Second

English translation copyright © 2019 by Dargaud Benelux (Dargaud-Lombard S.A.)

Published by First Second
First Second is an imprint of Roaring Brook Press,
a division of Holtzbrinck Publishing Holdings Limited Partnership
120 Broadway, New York, NY 10271

Don't miss your next favorite book from First Second!
For the latest updates go to firstsecondnewsletter.com and sign up for our enewsletter.

Library of Congress Control Number: 2020911190
Paperback ISBN: 978-1-250-62205-1
Hardcover ISBN: 978-1-250-62204-4

Our books may be purchased in bulk for promotional, educational, or business use.
Please contact your local bookseller or the Macmillan Corporate and Premium Sales Department
at (800) 221-7945 ext. 5442 or by email at MacmillanSpecialMarkets@macmillan.com.

American edition edited by Robyn Chapman
English translation by Montana Kane
Cover design by Kirk Benshoff
Interior design by Molly Johanson
Printed in China by Toppan Leefung Printing Ltd., Dongguan City, Guangdong Province

Originally written in Dutch and translated to French by Laurent Bayer
Originally published in 2019 in French by Dargaud as *Yasmina et les mangeurs de patates*
Previously published in 2019 by Europe Comics as two English e-books titled
*Yasmina and the Potato Eaters: Part 1* and *Yasmina and the Potato Eaters: Part 2*
Text and illustrations by Wauter Mannaert copyright © 2019 by Dargaud Benelux
(Dargaud-Lombard S.A.)–Mannaert

FIRST
EDITION

First American edition, 2021

Paperback: 10 9 8 7 6 5 4 3 2 1
Hardcover: 10 9 8 7 6 5 4 3 2 1

BY ART
WE LIVE